The Not-So-Tiny Tales of
Simon Seahorse

2

I Spy . . . a Shark!

By Cora Reef
Illustrated by Liam Darcy

LITTLE SIMON
New York   London   Toronto   Sydney   New Delhi

LITTLE SIMON
An imprint of Simon & Schuster Children's Publishing Division
1230 Avenue of the Americas, New York, New York 10020
First Little Simon paperback edition December 2021
Copyright © 2021 by Simon & Schuster, Inc.
All rights reserved, including the right of reproduction in whole or in part in any form.
LITTLE SIMON is a registered trademark of Simon & Schuster, Inc., and associated colophon is a trademark of Simon & Schuster, Inc. For information about special discounts for bulk purchases, please contact Simon & Schuster Special Sales at 1-866-506-1949 or business@simonandschuster.com.
The Simon & Schuster Speakers Bureau can bring authors to your live event. For more information or to book an event contact the Simon & Schuster Speakers Bureau at 1-866-248-3049 or visit our website at www.simonspeakers.com.
Designed by Leslie Mechanic
The text of this book was set in Causten Round.
Manufactured in the United States of America 1121 MTN
10 9 8 7 6 5 4 3 2 1
Library of Congress Cataloging-in-Publication Data
Names: Reef, Cora, author. | Darcy, Liam, illustrator.
Title: I spy... a shark! / by Cora Reef ; illustrated by Liam Darcy.
Other titles: I spy a shark!
Description: First Little Simon paperback edition. | New York : Little Simon, 2021. | Series: The not-so-tiny tales of Simon Seahorse ; #2 | Audience: Ages 5–9. | Audience: Grades K–1. | Summary: While exploring Coral Jungle, Simon Seahorse and his best friend Olive Octopus encounter a shark named Zelda who invites them to her mother's birthday party at Shark Point—and Simon not only has a unique school report, but the makings of an exciting story.
Identifiers: LCCN 2021017789 (print) | LCCN 2021017790 (ebook) | ISBN 9781665903707 (paperback) | ISBN 9781665903714 (hardcover) | ISBN 9781665903721 (ebook)
Subjects: LCSH: Sea horses–Juvenile fiction. | Octopuses–Juvenile fiction. | Sharks–Juvenile fiction. | Storytelling–Juvenile fiction. | CYAC: Sea horses–Fiction. | Octopuses–Fiction. | Sharks–Fiction. | Storytelling–Fiction.
Classification: LCC PZ7.1.R4423 Iap 2021 (print) | LCC PZ7.1.R4423 (ebook) | DDC [Fic]–dc23
LC record available at https://lccn.loc.gov/2021017789
LC ebook record available at https://lccn.loc.gov/2021017790

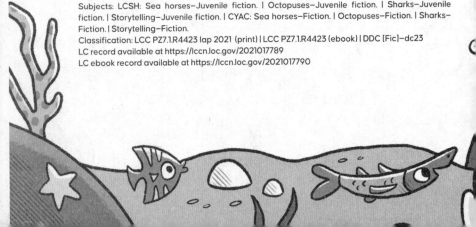

Contents

A Shark Tale

"So, Koto the shark kept swimming," Simon Seahorse said. "He was sure he was lost now."

Simon glanced around at his family to make sure everyone was paying attention. His siblings and his dad were spread out on bubble chairs in the living room.

They'd finished dinner and were now passing around a platter of kelp-chip cookies. Everyone was listening to Simon's story with wide eyes.

"Oh no!" said his youngest brother, Earl. "What is the shark going to do?"

"Just then," Simon went on, "Koto came upon something he'd never seen before. It was a huge shipwreck with tons of treasures! There were piles of golden coins and sparkling silver statues."

Lulu, Simon's second-youngest sibling, squealed with excitement. She loved anything shiny.

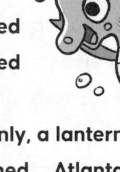

"Suddenly, a lantern fish named Atlanta came swimming out!" Simon cried.

"Oh!" Earl piped up. "Your friend Atlanta. You told us about him before."

Simon nodded and continued his story. "Atlanta knew the ocean better than anyone. And luckily for Koto,

Atlanta knew exactly how to get back
to Shark Point. So he showed Koto
the way home, and the shark lived
happily ever after. The end!"

Simon's brothers and sisters cheered. Since there were twelve children in the Seahorse family, the sound filled the entire house.

Simon leaned back, smiling. He loved to mix things from real life with ideas from his imagination when he told his stories. Koto might have been pretend, but Atlanta the lantern fish was real. Simon had met him at Shipwreck Station when he'd been looking for his lost pearl.

"Dad?" Lulu asked. "Are sharks as scary as they seem?"

"Well," Mr. Seahorse said slowly, "I've only met one shark in my life. . . ."

Everyone gasped, including Simon. How had he never heard about this before?

"Dad, you've *really* met a shark?" Earl asked.

"I really have," Mr. Seahorse said. "It was a long time ago, before any of you were hatched. Some friends and I were bubble jumping at Red Reef Springs when we saw him."

"What was he like?" Simon asked. "Were his teeth as sharp as swords? Did he try to swallow you up in one gulp?"

Mr. Seahorse laughed. "Actually, he was perfectly friendly. He had never been bubble jumping before, so we showed him how to do it. Then he said goodbye and made his way back to Shark Point!"

Simon frowned. That didn't sound right. Everyone knew sharks were the fiercest creatures in the entire ocean.

Still, it was pretty amazing his dad had met a real live shark!

Maybe if Simon were super lucky, he too would meet a shark one day. Imagine the stories he'd be able to tell then!

The Special Project

The next morning, Simon met his best friend, Olive Octopus, at the corner of Seaweed Lane before school.

"Hi, Simon!" Olive said. She checked the watches on each of her arms. "Wow, you're almost on time today!"

"Well, if I hadn't stopped to help a boxfish who'd gotten stuck in a very holey piece of coral, I *would* have been on time!" said Simon.

Olive laughed. "Sure you would have, Simon."

Olive loved a good story. But she also knew when to bring Simon back to reality. They were best friends, after all!

Together, the friends hopped into the current that would bring them to Coral Grove Elementary. Simon loved the current. It saved his small fins from having to work overtime to keep up with the larger sea creatures. Plus, it was fun!

"You'll never believe what my dad told me yesterday," Simon said to Olive.

"I bet I won't," Olive said with a smile.

Simon could tell Olive anything—even if it was completely made up. But this *wasn't* made up.

"He said he met a shark once!" Simon said.

Olive gasped. "Really?"

Simon nodded and told Olive what his dad had said: that the shark he'd met was nice!

"Hmm," Olive said. "That doesn't fit with what I've read about sharks. But I hope I *never* get a chance to find out." She shivered with fright.

Simon and Olive arrived at school and swam up the reef to Ms. Tuttle's classroom.

"Hey, watch where your tentacles are going!" someone cried.

Simon and Olive turned to find their classmate Cam Crab glaring at them. One of Olive's arms had accidentally gotten caught on Cam's claw.

"Sorry!" Olive said. "These things have a mind of their own sometimes."

Cam only grumbled as he scuttled away.

"*Someone* woke up on the wrong side of the clamshell this morning," Simon whispered.

Olive laughed as they headed into the classroom and found their seats.

"Good morning, everyone!" Ms. Tuttle said. "I'm thrilled to tell you about a special project we'll be working on. This week, you'll pick a place in or around Coral Grove to study and report back on."

Excited murmurs spread through the classroom, especially when Ms. Tuttle said they could work with a partner. Simon and Olive exchanged looks. They'd be working together, of course.

In the front row, Cam raised a claw. "Can I do a report on my house?" he asked. "It's definitely the most interesting place in Coral Grove."

Ms. Tuttle smiled. "You certainly can if you'd like. But why don't you spend a day or two thinking about it before you decide?"

Simon bounced with excitement. There were so many fantastic places in Coral Grove! Now they just had to pick one....

He was lost in thought when Olive suddenly poked him.

"Uh, Simon? It's time for art!" she said.

Simon realized that all his classmates were already swimming toward the art room. He followed them, his head still swirling with ideas.

Picking the
Perfect Place

Simon tried to focus during art, but his mind kept drifting. He wanted to come up with the *perfect* place for his project. One that would wow everyone.

Usually art was one of Simon's favorite classes. In art, he could truly let his imagination run wild.

But today he was so distracted
that even *he* thought his painting
looked more like melted kelpmallows
than it did the still life his teacher
had set up.

As he and Olive left school at the end of the day, Olive said, "I've already made a plan for our project. First, we pick a location. Then, we use our senses to observe everything we can. Then, we write a detailed report. Then, we give a fantastic presentation!"

"Sounds great, Olive," said Simon. "But *how* are we going to decide on a location? It has to be someplace no one else will report on. Maybe even someplace no one else has ever been!"

"How about we go back down to Shipwreck Station?" Olive suggested.

"We can visit Atlanta, and there's lots to report on there."

"True," Simon said. "But I did already tell everyone about Shipwreck Station."

"Hmm. How about Sea Star Cove?" Olive asked. "We haven't been there in ages."

"That would be a good one," Simon said, "but Lionel already picked it." Simon really wanted their presentation to be one of a kind.

"Well, we can always do our report on Cam's house," Olive joked.

"It *is* his favorite spot in Coral Grove," Simon said with a laugh. Then he gasped. "Wait! That's it!"

Olive frowned. "You really think we should use Cam's house for our project?"

"No!" Simon cried. "We should use *our* favorite spot."

Simon and Olive looked at each other. "Coral Jungle!" they said together.

Coral Jungle contained tons of different types of coral—maybe more than anywhere else in the ocean. A variety of fish and other sea creatures passed through every day. There were coral vines to swing from, coral slides to slide down, and even a coral flower patch to pick from. There would be plenty to study for their project. Plus, Simon couldn't remember ever seeing anyone else from school there.

"Remember last time we went to Coral Jungle to play I spy?" Simon said. "We almost got *blown away* when a sea turtle sneezed!"

Olive laughed. "I wouldn't say we almost got *blown away*. But I do remember that."

"If we're lucky, maybe it will happen again and we can put it in our report!" Simon said.

"We can head there after school tomorrow," Olive said, nodding. "I'll tell my mom not to expect me at the library."

Simon bounced with excitement. He couldn't wait to go to Coral Jungle. Who knew what they'd discover there this time?

I Spy...
a Shark!

The next day after school, Simon and Olive took the current all the way out to Coral Jungle.

When they arrived, they hopped out. The sight of Coral Jungle amazed Simon every time. It had to be the most colorful place in all of Coral Grove. There were sea pens and sea fans.

There was tree coral and fire coral. But Simon's favorite was the bubble coral, which puffed up with water during the day and then deflated at night. Simon had never been to Coral Jungle at night, but he

had learned about bubble coral in oceanography. Plus, it was a beautiful electric green.

"Let's start taking notes for our report," Olive said, pulling out a seaweed paper notebook.

"How about we play one tiny, little, quick round of I spy?" Simon suggested, holding his fins together pleadingly. "Then we can get to work."

Olive smiled. "All right. But we don't have time to *accidentally* get sneezed on by a sea turtle."

Simon shrugged. "If it happens, it happens," he said.

Olive glanced around. "I spy . . . a lionfish!" she announced, starting the game.

Because the jungle was so dense, Simon and Olive's game of I spy was more like a combination of I spy and hide-and-seek.

Simon pushed aside a sea fan. For a moment, he thought he spied the lionfish. But it was just another piece of coral. Then he saw a striped dorsal fin and knew right away.

"Found it!" Simon cried, pointing to the lionfish swimming by. "All right, my turn." He looked around carefully, taking his time to find something good. "I spy . . . a red urchin!"

Instantly, Olive sped off through the coral.

Simon smiled smugly to himself as Olive searched. The urchin was so well hidden, Simon thought he might have finally stumped her this time.

"Found it!" Olive suddenly cried, pointing to the urchin.

"Wow, I thought I had you!" said Simon. "Okay, let's each take one more turn."

"I spy . . . ," Olive began, still looking around. Then her mouth dropped open. "A shark!"

"You spy a shark?" Simon laughed. "Good one, Olive. If you don't want to play anymore, we can just start working on our report."

But when Simon looked at Olive again, he saw she'd gone from her normal bright pink to a pink paler than anything he'd ever seen in the ocean.

"Sh-sh-shark!" Olive stammered.
And that's when Simon saw it. Two
big eyes and an even bigger set of
teeth.

A Speedy Escape

Simon gasped. There was a real live shark right in front of them! She was even bigger than Simon had imagined a shark could be. And so were her teeth.

For a moment, Simon just stared in shock. Then Olive whimpered, and it snapped him back to reality.

They had to get away!

Simon grabbed one of Olive's arms with his tail, and they swam off as fast as they could. By the time they'd reached the outskirts of Coral Jungle, they were both breathing so heavily

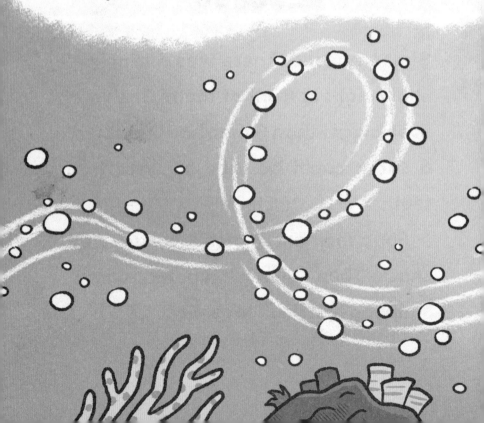

that bubbles enveloped them. They couldn't see anything.

Finally, the bubbles cleared. Simon glanced around. There was no sign of the shark. Phew! They'd lost her.

"Help!" Olive cried. Her arms were all twisted into a knot from swimming so fast. Simon hurried over and quickly helped her untangle them.

"I can't believe we just saw a shark," Simon said. "A *real* shark!"

"I thought sharks only lived in Shark Point," said Olive, her tentacles still trembling.

"Me too," said Simon. "I wonder what she was doing here."

"Well, I don't want to stick around to ask her," said Olive, stuffing her seaweed notebook into her satchel.

"Uh . . . ," said Simon. "We may not have a choice." He pointed toward Coral Jungle.

There was the shark, swimming toward them.

Simon frantically looked around for a place to hide, but they were in open water. There was nowhere to go.

The shark's eyes were focused right on the two small sea creatures. She was studying them as if deciding which one to eat first.

Simon and Olive slowly backed away, but the shark was bigger and faster than they were. As she reached them, she opened her mouth.

Simon covered his eyes with his fins. He couldn't bear to look! He huddled together with Olive, waiting for ... *something.*

But nothing happened.

Then Simon heard a surprisingly friendly voice. "Hi there!" said the shark.

A Shark
Named Zelda

Slowly, Simon peeled his fins away
from his eyes.

The shark was still there. But she
wasn't trying to gobble them up. Or at
least it didn't seem like she was. In fact,
it seemed like she was . . . smiling at
them? It was hard to tell with all those
huge, sharp teeth glinting in the light.

"Olive," Simon whispered, "I think you can open your eyes."

Olive opened her eyes, but she was still curled up, a ball of nerves.

"I'm Zelda!" the shark said. "Who are you?"

Simon felt as though his snout were glued shut. "I'm—I'm Simon," he said finally. "And this is Olive." He motioned to Olive, who was trying to hide behind him. Since Simon was smaller than she was, it wasn't working very well.

"Please—please don't eat us," Olive said.

Zelda didn't say anything for a moment. Then she started to laugh.

"Eat you?" Zelda said. "No offense, but you're not really my type. Plus, my

dad has a snack for me at home, and I don't want to ruin my appetite." She rubbed her belly with a fin.

Simon had never felt so relieved. Olive clearly felt it too, because she finally swam out from behind him.

"So . . . why are you here in Coral Jungle?" Simon asked. "I thought sharks only lived in Shark Point."

As Simon asked the question, he wondered: Was that just a myth? Created so that young sea creatures wouldn't be worried they might bump into a shark at any moment?

"Oh, I do live in Shark Point," Zelda said. "But I came to pick a bouquet of coral flowers for my mom. It's her birthday tomorrow. I heard Coral Jungle has the best flowers around."

Simon and Olive exchanged wide-eyed glances. A shark birthday party!

"But, honestly, I'm not very good at this," Zelda went on. "I don't know which coral flowers to pick, and I need to get back home before my mom does so I can hide the bouquet."

Hmm, thought Simon. *It sounds like Zelda needs our help.* "We know every type of coral around here," he said. "Do you want us to show you which ones to pick?"

Zelda smiled even wider than before. "Yes, I would love that!"

Olive gave Simon a hesitant look, then smiled nervously at Zelda and said, "F-follow us!"

As Simon and Olive led Zelda back into Coral Jungle, Simon's stomach fluttered. Could they really trust a shark? Or had he and Olive just made a big mistake?

But there was no turning back now. They'd never be able to swim out of Coral Jungle fast enough to get away. So Simon crossed his fins and reminded himself that this would make for a *really* good story!

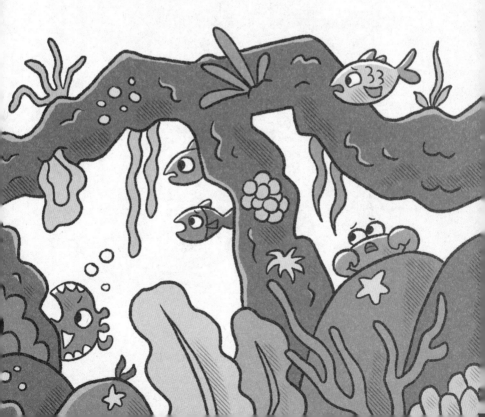

Surprise Invitation

Simon and Olive showed Zelda around Coral Jungle, pointing out all the best spots. They even told her about their favorite game.

"We never thought we'd spy a *shark* around here!" Simon said.

Finally, they stopped at the coral flower patch. It spread out before them, a rainbow of colors.

"This is the only area we're allowed to pick from," Olive explained.

"Wow, there are so many different kinds," Zelda said.

Simon noticed that she looked uncertain about where to begin, so he decided to start her off.

"Let's try some pink braided coral and a little bit of yellow stardust," he said, pulling them up with his tail. "Ooh, this peach blossom would go nicely with those."

"You really have an eye for this," Zelda said.

Simon smiled. "I love flowers and colors and, well, really anything that brightens someone's day!" When he was finished, he held out the bouquet, and Zelda accepted it with a smile. "Thank you," she said. "It's perfect. This will *definitely* brighten my mom's day!"

"Well, I guess we'll be going now," Olive said. "We still need to work on our project."

No matter how nice Zelda seemed, Simon could tell that Olive was still a little bit nervous around the shark.

"It was nice to meet you," Simon said. "See you around!" He couldn't wait to tell his family about this when he got home later.

"Wait!" Zelda said. "Have you two ever been to Shark Point?"

"Of course not!" Olive said, her eyes growing as round as sand dollars.

But Simon smiled.  "Well, we have in my stories," he said. "Remember, Olive? There's one about a shark who gets  lost. And another about the time I accidentally swam to Shark Point while I was following a shrimp. And another about the great shark magician."

Zelda laughed. "I have a feeling the Shark Point in your stories is probably more exciting than it is in real life," she said. "But I was wondering . . . do you want to come to my mom's birthday tomorrow? I'm sure she'd love to meet you two, and you can tell her all about the coral flowers in her bouquet."

"Uh, I'm not sure . . . ," Olive said.

But Simon couldn't pass up this chance to explore a whole new place. And suddenly he knew exactly why Olive would want to go too.

"Olive!" he cried. "We can do our report on Shark Point!"

Welcome to Shark Point!

The next day, Simon and Olive hopped on the current that Zelda had said would take them to Shark Point. In Coral Grove, the current often brought you right to your destination, but getting to Shark Point wasn't so easy. They were going to have to follow Zelda's directions exactly to find it.

"Okay," Olive said after they'd hopped out of the current. "Zelda told us that we'd pass a tall rock tower. Then we go past two patches of seagrass and turn right at the sand formation that looks like a shark."

Simon looked around. "That must be the rock tower," he said. "But are you sure it wasn't three patches of seagrass?" He was eager to visit Shark Point, but he did *not* want to get lost there.

"It was two," Olive said, checking the directions in her notebook. "Come on. I think it's this way."

As they swam, Simon's stomach bubbled with nerves and excitement. He clutched something tightly in his tail. It was a necklace he'd made for Zelda's mom out of seagrass and

shells. A guest couldn't show up to a birthday party without a gift, after all!

Meanwhile, Olive was taking notes for their project. "It's funny," she said when she was done writing. "This place doesn't feel that different from home, just a bit ... bigger."

Suddenly, something huge swam by—so huge that it carried Simon and Olive up with a wave.

"What was *that*?" Olive cried as she and Simon grabbed on to each other.

"Whatever it is, it's coming around again!" Simon said.

The creature came into view, and Simon gulped. It was a shark. And it wasn't Zelda.

"You must be Simon and Olive!" the shark said with a big grin. "I'm Zinc, Zelda's brother. Follow me. Zelda had to finish setting up for the party, but she's waiting for you!"

Simon and Olive exchanged nervous looks. Then, still holding on to each other, they followed Zinc. They passed cave after cave. Here and there shark heads popped out to get a look at the visitors.

"I've never seen so many caves," Olive said.

"In Shark Point, each shark family has a cave of their own," Zinc explained.

Simon was about to ask Zinc whether the water was truly colder here or if *he* was just cold, when the shark stopped suddenly.

"Hi there!" a familiar friendly voice said. It was Zelda. "Welcome to Shark Point."

Happy Birthday!

Simon and Olive swam into Zelda's family's cave. It was dark but lit up by twinkling lights all around.

"Wow, that's a great 'happy birthday' sign," Simon said. The words were spelled out in colorful shells.

Zelda grinned. "Thanks! I made it myself."

Deeper in the cave, two very large sharks were waiting. Simon and Olive both froze at the sight of them.

"Mom, Dad," Zelda said, "this is Simon, and this is Olive. They're the ones who helped me yesterday."

"So nice to meet you!" Zelda's dad said. He had the pointiest teeth Simon had ever seen. Simon reminded himself that surely Zelda wouldn't have led them here to be eaten.

"We're glad you could join us," Zelda's mom said.

"Happy birthday!" Simon told her. He held out the gift he'd made.

"What a beautiful bracelet," Zelda's mom said. "Thank you!"

Simon was about to tell her that it was actually a necklace, but then she put it around her fin. On her, he realized, it was a bracelet. "Uh, you're welcome," he said.

"We're about to have some kelp cake," Zelda's dad said. "Would you like some?"

"You eat kelp too?" Simon asked, surprised.

"I thought sharks ate other sea creatures like . . . like us!" Olive said.

Zelda and Zinc laughed.

"Not *all* sharks," Zelda said. "Around here we eat plants, just like you do."

Simon and Olive looked at each other. Surely no one in Coral Grove knew this—or sharks wouldn't be such mysterious creatures!

Everyone settled in around the table, and Simon dug into his giant slice of cake. He couldn't believe he was at a birthday party with an entire family of sharks.

"There's something I wanted to ask you," Simon said after he'd licked his plate clean. "Why *don't* sharks really leave Shark Point?"

"Yeah, why don't you come visit Coral Grove?" Olive asked.

Zelda shrugged. "We love it here in Shark Point," she said. "It's our home, just like Coral Grove is yours."

"Yeah, look at all this space we have," said Zinc. "No offense, but everything in Coral Grove is *tiny.*"

Simon laughed. "I guess I never thought about it like that," he said.

"Zinc and I do like to explore new areas sometimes," said Zelda. "That's how I heard about Coral Jungle.

Oh, that reminds me! Simon, do you want to tell my mom about all the coral flowers you picked?"

"Sure!" said Simon. "But first, let me tell you about the time I picked what I *thought* was a coral flower . . . and turned out to be a sea slug!"

The Final Report

On the day of the presentations, Ms. Tuttle's classroom was bustling with activity. Some students had written papers, some had collected objects from the place they'd studied, and some had even created dioramas.

Simon and Olive had made a factual poster board about Shark Point.

They would also act out some scenes from their meeting with Zelda and her family. Olive wasn't so sure the second part was necessary . . . but Simon was certain it would give their presentation a little something extra.

As Nix finished her report on Seagrass Fields, Simon wiggled in his seat. He and Olive were up next.

Ms. Tuttle called on them, and they headed to the front of the classroom.

"Our presentation," Simon began, "is on Shark Point."

The entire class gasped.

Cam immediately raised a claw. "Ms. Tuttle, aren't we supposed to present on a place we've actually been?"

"We *have* been there!" Simon said.

"And we have this to prove it." Olive held up a piece of coral. "This type of silver coral only grows in Shark Point."

Ms. Tuttle smiled and motioned for them to continue.

As Olive narrated facts about Shark Point, Simon acted out their meeting with Zelda. When he pretended to be Olive with her arms all tangled into a knot, everyone giggled, including Olive.

When their report was finished, the whole class clapped. Even Cam.

"Wonderful work," Ms. Tuttle said.

As Simon headed back to his seat, Lionel stopped him and whispered, "Could you take me to Shark Point sometime?"

"Maybe one day!" Simon told him.

But he and Olive exchanged knowing looks. The truth was, they had promised Zelda that they'd keep the directions to Shark Point a secret.

There was a reason you couldn't just hop on a current and arrive there. And the sharks preferred it that way. But Zelda had promised she'd find a way for them to meet again.

After the reports were finished, the class hurried out to the playground. As Simon and Olive jumped onto the swings, a group of friends crowded around them.

"Tell us more about Shark Point!" Nix said.

Olive turned to Simon and smiled.

"This one is all yours," she said.

Simon smiled back, his mind already swirling with ideas. "Well, it all started with a game of I spy," he began.

SIMON'S STORY

Once upon a time, there was a shark named Zelda. She was a super nice shark, but anytime she tried to make a friend, the sea creature would swim away in fear. One day, a seahorse named Simon was underwater surfing. He

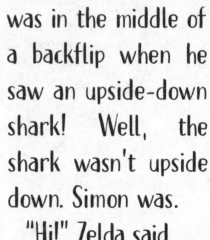

was in the middle of a backflip when he saw an upside-down shark! Well, the shark wasn't upside down. Simon was.

"Hi!" Zelda said.

Simon was surprised, but not scared. "Hi!" said Simon.

"Do you want to play a game?" asked Zelda.

"Sure!" said Simon. "I've always wanted to be friends with a shark."

Zelda was so happy, she tossed Simon into the air so high that he flew *out* of the water and then came diving back down. "That was totally awesome!" said Simon. Zelda knew that they were going to be best friends.

THE END

Here's a peek at Simon's next big adventure!

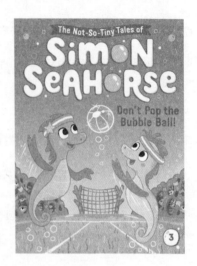

"You won't believe what happened today!" Simon Seahorse said as he unpacked his backpack after school.

"Did you meet another shark?" his younger brother, Earl, asked.

"Did you lose your lucky pearl

An excerpt from *Don't Pop the Bubble Ball!*

again?" his little sister, Lulu, wanted to know.

A few of Simon's older siblings glanced over from the kitchen table. Simon was one of twelve brothers and sisters, so he always had an audience.

"Close!" Simon said with a laugh. But just as he was about to launch into one of his incredible tales, his oldest sister, Kya, burst into the house. She was out of breath, and her favorite Deep-Sea Divers cap hung sideways off her head.

An excerpt from *Don't Pop the Bubble Ball!*

"Wow, and I thought I knew how to make an entrance," Simon joked. "Were you being chased by a tiger shark? Or an octopus with eight legs *and* eight heads?"

Kya grinned. "Even better," she said. "I just found out bubble ball tryouts are this weekend!"

"That's great, Kya," Mr. Seahorse said. A few of Simon's siblings nodded in agreement, but no one seemed as excited as Kya. They were all busy with homework or other projects.

Kya's face fell. "Doesn't anyone *care*?" she asked.

An excerpt from *Don't Pop the Bubble Ball!*